Norman Plays Basketball

by CLARE and FRANK GAULT

Pictures by BERNICE MYERS

SCHOLASTIC BOOK SERVICES
NEW YORK · TORONTO · LONDON · AUCKLAND · SYDNEY · TOKYO

No part of this publication may be reproduced in whole or in part, or stored in a retrieval system, or transmitted in any form or by any means, electronic, mechanical, photocopying, recording, or otherwise, without written permission of the publisher. For information regarding permission, write to Scholastic Book Services, 50 West 44th Street, New York, NY 10036.

Copyright © 1978 by Clare S. Gault and Frank M. Gault. Illustrations copyright © 1978 by Bernice Myers. All rights reserved. Published by Scholastic Book Services, a division of Scholastic Magazines, Inc.

12 11 10 9 8 7 6 5 4 3 2 1   2   8 9/7 0 1 2 3/8

Printed in the U.S.A.

07

For our son Dave, basketball and football player,
writer, and always a big help.

Norman's father put up a
basketball hoop behind their garage.
And for months, Norman went there
by himself.
He practiced shooting baskets.
He practiced dribbling.

"This year, I've got to make the team,"
Norman said.

But when teams were picked at Norman's
school, Norman was left out.
His friends — Hound Dog Calhoun,
Rabbit Wilson, Pounce Paulsen, Stinky Martin,
and Muskrat Monroe — were all on the Braves.

"Hey, fellas," Norman said. "What about me?"

"Gee, Norman," Muskrat said. "We need players who can run fast. We'd like to have you on our team, but I'm afraid you wouldn't be able to keep up with our fast plays."

"Oh," Norman said.

"Wait a minute," Stinky said. "Why not let Norman be our extra player, just in case someone gets sick or hurt."

"Thanks, fellas," said Norman. "I'll do my best."

So Norman joined the team. He took care of their equipment and cheered them from the bench.

The Braves were a good team and they started winning right away.

In between games,
Norman practiced with
the rest of the team.

Another school had a team called the Roughnecks.
They were big and tough, and they were hard
to beat. Weasel Warren was their captain.

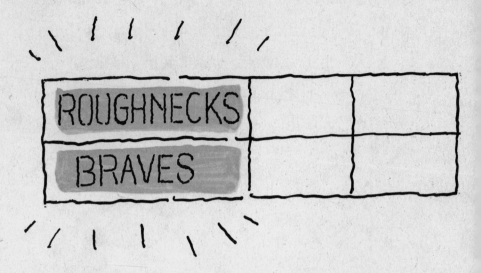

Now it was the end of the season.
The Braves had to
play the Roughnecks.
The winners would be champions.

The big game started.
Norman cheered his team from the bench.

The Braves made the first basket on a fast play — Rabbit Wilson to Hound Dog to Stinky Martin. Stinky jumped and put the ball into the hoop. It was an easy lay-up for two points.

The Roughnecks came right back and made a
basket. They were so big, the Braves couldn't
stop them.

The game was a see-saw battle.
First the Braves made a basket.
Then the Roughnecks made a basket.

When the game was half over, the score
was tied, 32 to 32.

Weasel Warren was upset. "Those Braves are
running all around us," he said to his team.
"We have to slow them down."

The buzzer sounded and the second half began.

Weasel and his teammates tried blocking the
Braves on their fast plays, but the Braves
were too quick.

Finally, when the referee wasn't looking,
Weasel stuck out his foot and tripped
Hound Dog as he ran past.

Hound Dog fell down — splat.

Poor Hound Dog. He got full of splinters from
the wood floor. He had to leave the game.

There were only a couple of minutes left in the game and the score was tied, 55 to 55.

Muskrat called time-out. "There's nothing we can do," he said to his team. "We have to bring Norman in."

"Now we've got 'em."

Weasel rubbed his hands together.

"They will never be able to run a fast play
with Norman in there."

Right away, the Roughnecks went to Norman's part of the court and shot over him for a basket.

Roughnecks 57, Braves 55.

Norman was slow, but he was able to dribble
the ball and protect it with his shell.
He got near the basket.

"Don't worry, team," Weasel laughed.
"Norman can't shoot."

Norman was in a good spot to shoot, but he was afraid he might miss. He decided to pass the ball to Stinky instead...

...but one of the Roughnecks caught the ball and
ran down the court to score a basket.

Roughnecks 59, Braves 55.

Muskrat called time-out
for a huddle.
"Norman, they aren't
guarding you.
They think you can't shoot."

"I know," Norman said.
"And that gives me
an idea."

Norman whispered something to his teammates.

The game started again. Norman had the ball. No one was guarding him.

Norman took a shot. The ball went very high into the air.

Rabbit jumped. He caught
the ball in midair,
and dropped it into the basket.
It was a perfect alley-oop play.

"Nice going, Norman!" the Braves shouted.

The Roughnecks missed their next shot.
Norman had the ball again.

"Watch out for that high shot!" Weasel yelled.

But this time Norman threw the ball low.

The pass was to Stinky Martin,
who jumped and put
the ball
through the hoop.

The score was tied again, 59 to 59.

Weasel was mad. "That's twice Norman fooled us."

The Roughnecks made a basket and were
ahead again.
Only seconds were left in the game.
Norman had the ball.

"No more of these tricky plays," Weasel said
to himself. "I'll stop Norman this time."

Just as Norman was ready to shoot,
Weasel jumped high to block the shot.

But he jumped too high. He lost his balance
and knocked Norman down. It was a foul.

The referee blew his whistle.
"Norman gets two foul shots," he said.

The score was Roughnecks 61, Braves 59.
Two foul shots would just tie the score.

The teams lined up for the foul shots. Norman
went to the foul line to shoot.

Only three seconds were left in the game.
The Braves needed both points or they would
lose the game.

Norman was very nervous.
His team
was depending
upon him.
He took aim.
He shot.

The ball bounced
off the backboard,
rolled around the rim...

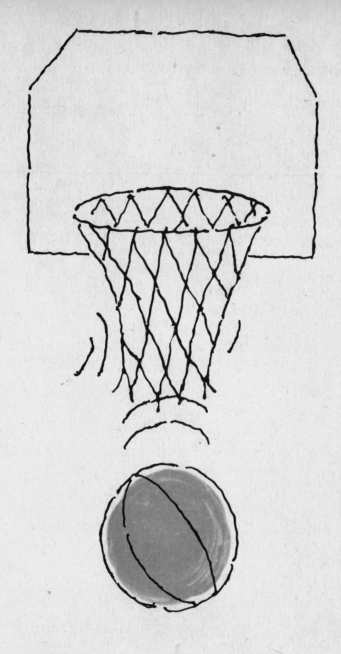

...and finally dropped in.

Roughnecks 61, Braves 60.

Weasel ground his teeth.

Then suddenly he smiled.

He thought of another trick.

This time he would really upset Norman.

Norman took aim for his second foul shot.
But just as he was shooting, Weasel let out
a loud sneeze. The noise made Norman jerk.
He pushed the ball too hard.

The ball went straight at the basket.
It hit the front of the rim hard...

...and the ball bounced right back at Norman.

Norman turned fast. His shell hit the ball and bounced it over to Pounce Paulsen.

Pounce grabbed the ball.
He jumped and put it
through the hoop just as
the final buzzer sounded.

It counted as a regular basket. Two points!

The Braves had won, 62 to 61.

"Quick thinking, Norman!" yelled Muskrat.

"Hooray for Norman!" shouted the Braves.

Norman was the hero of the basketball team.

Norman is the hero of other books too.
You may want to read them.

You may also want to read these sports books by Clare and Frank Gault:

The Day the Stars Played the Monsters
  pictures by Bernice Myers

The Harlem Globetrotters and Basketball's Funniest Games, pictures by Charles McGill

The Cartoon Book of Sports, pictures by
  Charles McGill

All these books are published in paperback by Scholastic Book Services.